THE
INVASION
D1048786

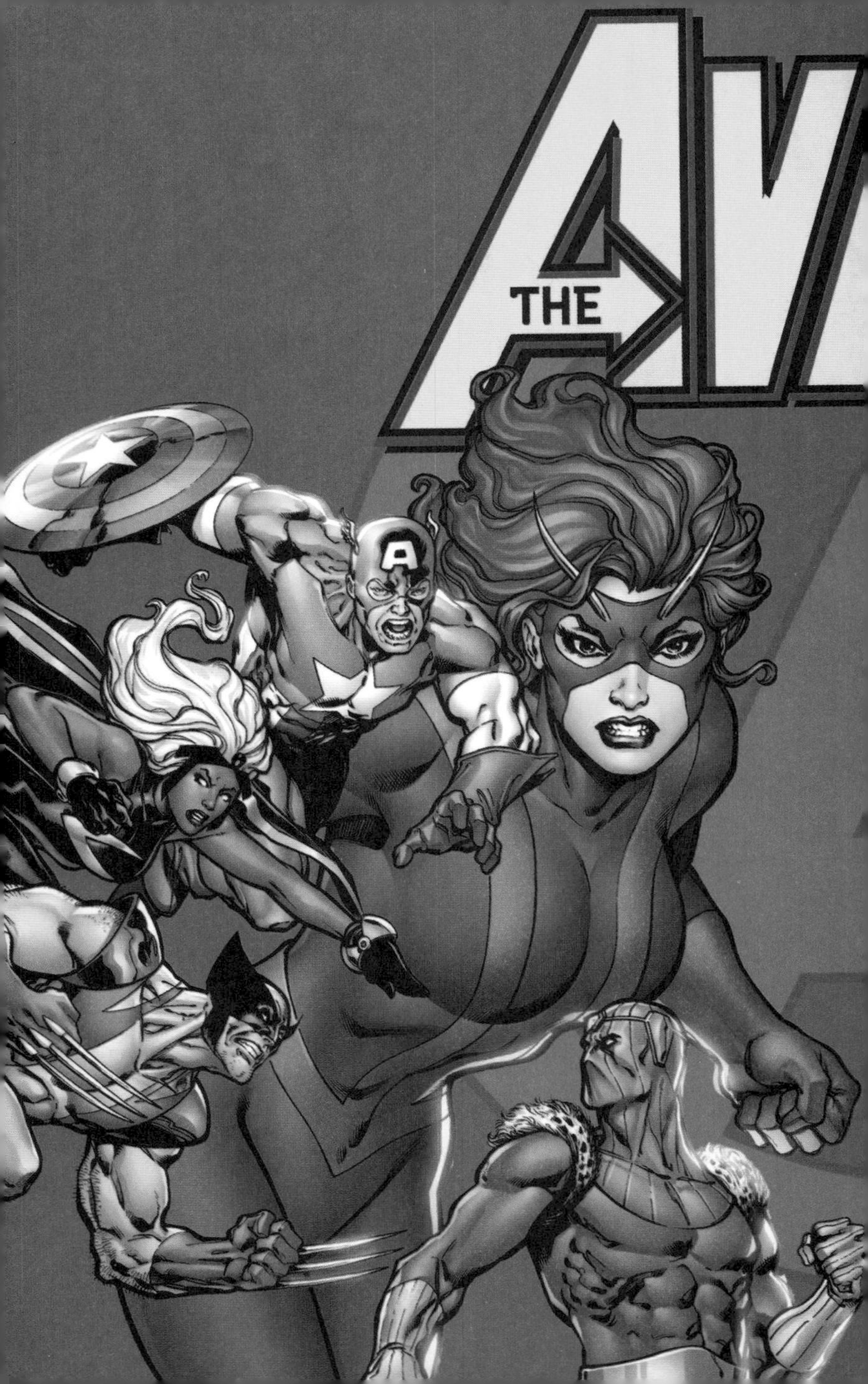
THE

NGERS

## INVASION

Writer: Paul Tobin
Pencils: Jacopo Camagni, Dario Brizuela
& Horacio Domingues
Inks: Jacopo Camagni, Leandro Corral
& Craig Yeung

Colors: Sotocolor
Letters: Dave Sharpe
Cover Art: Ig Guara & Sotocolor; David Williams
& Sean Galloway; and Casey Jones & Sotocolor
Consulting Editor: Ralph Macchio
Editor: Nathan Cosby

Captain America created by Joe Simon & Jack Kirby

Collection Editor: Cory Levine
Assistant Editors: Alex Starbuck & John Denning
itors, Special Projects: Jennifer Grünwald & Mark D. Beazley
Senior Editor, Special Projects: Jeff Youngquist
Senior Vice President of Sales: David Gabriel
Vice President of Creative: Tom Marvelli

Editor in Chief: Joe Quesada
Publisher: Dan Buckley
Executive Producer: Alan Fine

#36

v York City...
Thinking 'bout sprucing up the ol' castle?
Nay. Not with this.
Yon haunted eyes follow Thor everywhere.
I need them.
You need commemorative Captain America and Bucky salt and pepper shakers?
Yes. I need them.
But don't you think--
I need them!
ee if there any Edgar Burroughs novels.
50%
Nothing. Just romance novels.
Oh, wait. Mickey Spillane.
It's beautiful.
Little dirty though.
Could I see that necklace please?
TREET FAIR
Awww... that'll probably rub right off.

RUB RUB RUB
Free! Free! Free at last!
After centuries of entrapment, Brank the genie tastes freedom at last!
Oh golly.
TIGRA
STORM
IRON MAN
WHICH WISH?!
CAT-LIKE CRUSADER. FERAL MUTANT BRAWLER. WEATHER GODDESS. SPIDER-POWERED WEB-SLINGER. BRILLIANT ARMORED INVENTOR. TOGETHER THEY ARE THE WORLD'S MIGHTIEST HEROES, BATTLING THE FOES THAT NO SINGLE SUPER HERO COULD WITHSTAND!
THE AVENGERS
PAUL TOBIN WRITER
JACOPO CAMAGNI ARTIST
SOTOCOLOR COLORS
DAVE SHARPE LETTERS
GUARA & SOTO COVER
PAUL ACERIOS PRODUCTION
RALPH MACCHIO CONSULTING
NATHAN COSBY EDITOR
JOE QUESADA EDITOR IN CHIEF
DAN BUCKLEY PUBLISHER
ALAN FINE EXECUTIVE PRODUCER

And you, my liberator, have earned three wishes!
Name them! Quickly!
Three... wishes?
I'll give you ten dollars for one of your wishes.
Tigra is not so irresponsible as to give you a wish. Further, ten dollars? She could simply wish for a good deal more.
Umm. Umm. Umm.
Wait, is this real? You're a enie? A three-wish genie?
This woman is trying my patience.
Tigra?
You okay?
You home?
SNAP
SNAP
SNAP

Does this one speak?
Normally. Kind of a lot, actually.
Don't take that the wrong way.
My patience is at an end! I have a task which needs doing!
Tigra! Make some wishes! Ten million dollars for all your friends!
Just say it!
Brank can wait no longer!
I must have my vengeance from the evil green ogre who trapped me, centuries ago!
You shall have your wishes in time, mute one, but I now thirst for retribution.
I go off to bring Brank's justice to the creature known as--
...the Incredible Hulk.
Uh-oh.

Okay, well, at's no good. This could be trouble.
Or it could be fun.
A magical creature just went off to fight the Hulk. We have to do something.
Our first task is to locate the Hulk, immediately.
He's not answering his communicator.
Thor and I will begin the search.
Try the petting zoo. Hulk loves it there.
Wait a second! We ave a quick fix!
Tigra, just make a wish that the genie doesn't want to fight the Hulk!
No. Way. No way!
Why not?
Guys...genie literature is filled with examples of wishes gone wrong.
If I wish for ten million dollars, it will probably fall from the sky and crush me!
If I wish for a pony, I'll probably get an evil Tigra-eating monster-pony!
If I wish for the genie not to fight the Hulk, then the genie will twist the words in some way and it will be worse!
These wishes are dangerous. Genie wishes always backfire!
Actually, she has a point.

Yo! I've got Bruce on the line.
I'll bring him up on holo-speak.
Hey everyone. What's with the priority call?
You've got a genie chasing after you. He's mad at the Hulk.
No, seriously. I'm busy here.
It is true, Bruce.
A genie, really?
How come you believe Storm, but not me?
Did you n just answ that all yoursel

Tigra accidentally set a genie free from some sort of magic necklace, and the genie blames the Hulk for trapping him there.
Know anything about it?
Not a thing. Are you sure he said Hulk?
He even said Incredible Hulk.
That's you, Bruce. Sorry!
We'll swing back to Avengers Tower and talk. Meet you there, okay?
Sure. See you in a bit.

We taking he quinjet, or should we--
--ulp!
This way's faster.
You taxi drivers are getting pushy.
We have to get there as quickly as possible. In terms of strength the Hulk can't be matched, but who knows what that genie can do?
Push these winds to the limit, Storm. I'm itching for a good scrap.
The wind is nearly hurricane force already. We'll be at the Tower in seconds.
Oh no!
What?
Some-thing just went crashing through the top window!
Your eyes must be amazing! Even with my binocular vision I can't...oh. I see it!
It's Bruce!

Storm! Your winds! Can you--?
I can.
This will slow his descent!
But he was hurled with such force! I am not sure I can stop him in time!
Tigra!
Got him!
Made it!
Is he conscious?

No. He has a bruise on-- oh golly!
What are you--
Aww, dang.

KABOOM
Move!
It's Brank!

So! You are all friends of the shape-changer?
Then you are my enemies!
Shape-hanger
He means Bruce. Or Hulk. Whichever.

You are so quick, furry one!
All thanks to my past intense training sessions combined with my current intense fear!
So tell me, what do you have against the Hulk, anyway?
Uhnnnn.
The Hulk?
Yes. It w almost f hundre years a
The Hulk, evilly disguised as Bruce Banner, had traveled back in time from the year 2021.
2021? Wait, tha not for years y So you're blami Bruce for somethi he did in the futu Or, would that b in the past?
I guess that makes days of futu past!
I was at the height of my fame. Many came from thousands of leagues to beg my favors.
In return, I required only a few small trinkets.

All was perfect, until the shape-changer arrived.
The shape-changer challenged me to a duel. If I lost, I was to be confined in the amulet. If he lost, then he would be my slave for all time.
I had acquired many slaves in just such a manner.
This match, I thought, was laughable. The shape-changer challenged me, me, to a duel of strength!
But I did not know his secret.
And that secret doomed me to five hundred years within the cursed amulet!

So I do all this in the past?
Yeah, but you don't travel back to the past for several years yet, apparently.
Sounds like something to look forward to.
Tigra, I still say you should just use one of your three wishes to make this whole mess go away!
Wait a minute! Did the genie give you wishes?
Yes.
Then use them!
Right! We're in trouble here!
Yeah! C'mon!
I don't want "Got his tuchas handed to him by a trash can" on my tombstone!
CRASH
No! Magical wishes are too dangerous.
I wish you all would understand that!

Granted.
Wait, Tigra's right.
Yeah...using magical wishes is kind of risky.
You are wise to play this so carefully, Tigra.
Huh?
We probably shouldn't take any chances with these wishes.
Storm's right...don't take the chance of a wish backfiring.

Besides, we can deal with this some other way!

What is this power?!! Have I gone mad?
Are you all magicians and ogres?

Ogre, huh?
SNIKT
Well, I've been called worse.

No. We will *not* now battle.
It is clear you are more *powerful* adversaries than I first believed. I must *reassess* the *means* of my *revenge!*
He's *vanished!*
Well, *now* what?
I do not believe we have seen the *last* of the genie.
Right. And thoughts are we should t lure him *out* the city, whe *innocents* be *hurt*
What category am *I* in? I mean...am I one of the *not-be-hurt innocents,* or that *other* category?
You're a fulltime *hero.* That's what *you* are.
Ahh. Dang.
I have a small house in the Catskills. Let's use that for headquarters.
Later that night...
*This* is a *small* house?

Yes. It's one of the smaller ones I own.
Now have a good night.

our wish becoming ueen is... ranted.
ad oh en!

Your wish of being stronger than the Hulk is... granted.
Oh, shoot!

Your wish of being loved by everyone is... granted.
I love her more than you do!
No! I love her the most!
You don't deserve her!

Your wish for the power of flight is... granted.
HA HA HA HA HA HA HA
But now you can never land!
HA HA HA HA HA HA

Morning...
Hey, where did all the *sausages* go?
Huh? *All* of them?
*Wolverine* ate them all.

Morning, Tigra. *Sleep* okay?
Wuz awake *all night.* Still s-sleepy.

What's for breakfast?
Eggs and sausage. Except we don't have any *sausage.*
Why not?

Because *Wolverine* ate them all.
That *jerk!* I wish he hadn't done that.
FWWUM

Oh geez.
Man, I'm hungry.
Anyone have a really good plan on how to deal with the genie?
Perhaps we should consult with Dr. Strange, or someone else who knows the mechanisms of magic?
That guy creeps me out.
You think it would help if I apologized to this genie?
Naww. Not when you still haven't done what you'd be apologizing for.
Good. Because I don't feel like apologizing.
Actually, when I asked if anyone had any plans on how to deal with the genie, I meant right now.

Outside! Now!

his time,
engeance
s mine!
r what you just
to my insurance
emiums, I think
ngeance should
be mine!
Normally
I'd tell you to
calm down,
Bruce...
...but this
time, go
for it!
RRRAGGHH!
Unnff!
Okay,
jawbreaker,
let's go
get--
WHHHH
THOOOM
SO, shape-
changer! You
show your true
colors at
last!!

Stay clear, Tigra. Let US handle this!
You kidding?! I'm an Avenger!
First...a quick stop in a tree.
And now, a quick kick to the head!
Ahhh! What?
Raaghh!!
He doesn't seem to be tangible when we try to touch him!
But I assure you, I am tangible when I touch you!
He...he's changing me back from the Hulk!
I didn't think anyone could do that!

He's got the dang trees attacking us now!!
Maybe we should have called Dr. Strange! This isn't really our kind of fight!
Stay away from the trees! I've got them!
Ha! That's right! We've got lightning!
Those dumb trees should have known better!
Tigra! Look out!
THWAMM
THWAMMK
They're too fast!
There's too many of them!
AHHH!

I wish for a magic genie-capturing lamp that never fails, works instantly, and traps genies for all time without causing any harm to anyone else!
What?!
NOOOOOOOOOOOOOOOO
Ha! Take that, Brank!
I'll see you later. Or, hundreds of years earlier. Well... whatever.
Looks like everything worked out okay.
My house.
And hopefully, we'll never have to worry about Brank again.
At least, wish

#37

CAPTAIN AMERICA
SPIDER-MAN
WOLVERINE
MISS AMERICA
GOLDEN GIRL
ORIGINAL HUMAN TO
TORO
SUB-MARI
WHIZZE
Avengers! We need to take down the Invaders without hurting them!
Cap, I'm not sure we can take down these guys at all!
Hit 'em HARD, Invaders!
We do battle for our glorious leader...the PUPPET MASTER!
DOLL WINNERS SQUAD
SUPER-SOLDIER FROM WORLD WAR II. SPIDER-POWERED WEB-SLINGER. FERAL MUTANT BRAWLER. AMERICAN WOMAN. GIRL OF GOLD. TOGETHER THEY ARE THE WORLD'S MIGHTIEST HEROES, BATTLING THE FOES THAT NO SINGLE SUPER HERO COULD WITHSTAND!
THE AVENGERS
PAUL TOBIN WRITER
DARIO BRIZUELA PENCILER
LEANDRO CORRAL INKER
SOTOCOLOR COLORISTS
DAVE SHARPE LETTERER
WILLIAMS & GALLOWAY COVER
PAUL ACERIOS PRODUCTION
RALPH MACCHIO CONSULTING
NATHAN COSBY EDITOR
JOE QUESADA EDITOR IN CHIEF
DAN BUCKLEY PUBLISHER
ROBOTIC MAN ON FIRE. ROBOTIC TEEN SIDE-KICK ON FIRE. ANGRY, ALIENATED UNDERWATER MONARCH. FASTER THAN PROCESSED CHEESE. TOGETHER THEY ARE THE WORLD'S MIGHTIEST HEROES, BATTLING THE FOES THAT NO SINGLE SUPER HERO COULD WITHSTAND!
THE INVADERS

he year 1954...
Thanks for coming over, Madeline.
Absolutely. You sounded very concerned.
It does, I'm afraid. Would you like some tea? Muffins?
Does it have anything to do with the recent disappear-ances?
Both, please. Now, should we start puzzling on these disappearances, or wait for Captain America? You did say your partner was showing up, right?
Well, ummm...he's certainly been worried about his friends.
He even started in on the case, but he and Bucky had to go off on some secret mission. Something about Baron Zemo.
Let's go ahead, then. And if Cap gets back in time, he can atch up. Or, in Captain America's case, he'll probably know more than we do.
Uhhh, right. So it all started when the Sub-Mariner went missing from his undersea kingdom.
I'm not sure that's a bad thing. He's a testy one, isn't he?
True, and if this was an isolated incident, then perhaps we'd leave it alone, but Cap got a phone call from Toro.
The Human Torch's partner?
Right. He said that the Torch had gone missing. Then, when I went to talk with Toro, he was nowhere to be found!
That's strange. It sounds like more than a coincidence.

What does Captain America think of all this?
Keep this very quiet, but Cap and Bucky have gone missing as well.
Captain America is... gone?
Oh my gosh!
KRINGG
KRINGG
Oh! The doorbell! That
be the Whizze
called him becau
this could all
a conspirac
against the
Invaders!
Afternoon, Golden Girl. I got here as fast as I could.
And for me, that's pretty--
Oh!
He's gone!
There's some sort of odd disturbance here in the air! My hand just disappears!

This might be our *only chance!*
You mean...?
*Yes!* Let's go *through* and see--
present day.
--what happens?
PASTE POT'S PIZZA!
POT'S
iss America? olden Girl? How d *you two* get here?
*Ahh!* I understand. You must ave been *near the Whizzer* during my *gathering.*
Who *are* you?
Why, my dear...I'm the *Puppet Master.*
Whizzer? *Whizzer?*
He's not *responding!*
*Of course* he's responding, but *only to me!*
*Whizzer! Subdue them!*

Oh my gosh! The Whizzer's being controlled!
We have to stop him!
Stop him how? He's too fast! It's like fighting lightning!
Worse! Lightning supposedly never strikes the same area twice, but I think I've already taken about a hundred punches!
Don't harm them too much, my puppet!
In a few moments more they will be under my control. I had planned to activate their puppets tomorrow, but why put it off?
The girls are here, the dolls are here, and opportunity is knock knock knocking! What a beautiful day!
The dolls! He's controlling the Whizzer with the doll!
He has dolls of the other Invaders, too! And...us!
Get those dolls!

block away...
We all have to do community service, even you. It's written in the Avengers charter.
Then charter me a plane to some-where else. Community service ain't my style.
PASTE POT'S PIZZA!
You could give the talk to Ms. Tardiff's third grade class.
The only topics I know ain't fit for teaching kids.
Got a point, there. How about helping run the hospital's blood drive?
Which is eduled for the ne time as my lby finals. No can do.
You could help the library move their stock to the new location.
With my fines, I ain't stepping near the library.
I'd suggest the Wee Scouts bake sale, but I seem to recall you eating about half their stock last year.
Yeah. I did. But I paid for them.
Not really. You stuck Tony Stark with the bill.
'm telling you, mmunity service st ain't my bag.
The public's perception of the Avengers is important. Being visible, doing community good, is imperative if we're going to--
AHHHHHHHHHH!
Hah! Hear that? Saved by the wail!

It was just around the corner here, I think.
Be ready for anything! With the recent upsurge in super villain activity, we could be facing--
Golden Girl?
Cap!
You know her?
She's... she's--
Snap out of it, chuckles! There's somebody speedy running around, too fast to be seen, and I don't think he's--
SSSSSSTHWWWAMM
Unggh!

Oh! Captain America! Then the Puppet Master must have kidnapped you as well!
--on our side.

Why is that woman throwing garbage into the air? And who are you?
Huh? Me? I'm the Golden Girl... Captain America's partner!
And she's throwing garbage into the air to make it harder for the Whizzer to move so fast!

ha ha!
You can't be serious! That's really his name?
Why are you laughing?
Golden Girl!
Uh! Good to see you, too, Cap!

WHABAM!
It's been so long! I can't believe it!
Huh? It's been no more than a week! You went off to fight Baron Zemo and then--

Getting pummeled over here!
We'll catch up later!
For now, what's all this about?
We were following the leads on those disappearances, like you said before you left, and the Whizzer was kidnapped. Mind-washed.
The disappearances? I'm trying to remember. It was all so long ago.
It has something to do with those puppets!
Oh, ehhh? Hello.
PASTE POT'S PIZZA
The Puppet Master.
I hate that guy.
Whizzer! These men are your primary targets!
Uggh

We have to help him!
Believe me, he'll heal! Our target is the Puppet Master!
PASTE POT'S PIZZA!
No! The dolls!
I'm not ready for this. If only I'd thought to bring the rest of the Invaders along, it would certainly be different.
But, for now... Whizzer, a bit of Captain America's hair, if you please.
Uhhh!
Ouch!
He's getting away!
Ease up. No way for us flatfoots to catch him.

Now, how did you get here?
Same as you, I guess.
I hardly think you were caught in an explosion and then frozen in a block of ice for several decades.

Ummm, no. We stepped through some sort of disturbance in the air.
Like a doorway, but invisible.

Hold on. A block of ice? Were you serious?
He was. Cap was found near Alaska, when--

Ahhh!
Easy. That's Spider-Man. He's an Avenger, like me.
Like... you? What's an Avenger?
Hmmm. You don't know where you are, do you?

New York, I thought? Right?
Yes. But, here...come over this way.
You're not in the 1950's anymore.
Oh. My. Goodness.
Wow. Such language.

o hours
ter, at
engers
wer...
So, we traveled through time somehow. Does this Puppet Master guy control time?
Not ever. At least not before.
Puppet Master is kind of a lame name.
cough Whizzer cough.
"The Puppet Master creates
puppets from a special radio-
active clay, with which he has
ome sort of mysterious bond.
"By adding a sample of a
erson's hair or tissue, he
control that person and
ce them to do his bidding!"
Oh no! Is
at why he had
he Whizzer
teal a lock of
your hair?
Infortunately,
an't think of any
other reason.
Maybe
e's just a big fan.
probably already
s your autograph,
action figure,
trading cards...
...underwear, toothpaste...
So the question is...how did he reach back in time to bring you here? And what's he up to?
He seemed surprised when we showed up, but not overly surprised. And he already had our dolls.
Cap's is pretty good!
We have to discover the Puppet Master's plans. I'll have Iron Man and Giant Girl stay behind, work the computer trail.
The rest of us should split up and see what we can find. But keep in contact, okay?
Right! Everyone, remember to bring a bunch of dimes for the pay phones!

One hour later...
How was I to know about these keen cell phones? What else should I know about the future?
By future, you mean the present, right? Because all I know about the future is that I'll be hungry around seven o'clock.
So, have we colonized space yet?
No. But space keeps trying to colonize us. This town has more alien invasions than...
...oh, hold on. There's the woman we're waiting for.
Hey! Whuh?
Miss America, meet Carolyn Detroit
underworld's number one gossip. She's
to tell us everything she knows abo
the Puppet Master.
Hey Spider-Ma
Hey, all I know is
he's been brag
about how he'll
own the past

And because of that, hey, we'll all have to bow down to him in today's world.
It's the usual King of the World stuff we get from these guys, but hey, he seems pretty confident.
Hey, you know your webbing leave
stains on sil
right?

hundred and thirty-six blocks away.
Ackkkk!
Ah, come on, Wolverine!
KRASSSH
We've told you everything we know.
The Puppet Master has some weird new time power! Wants to use it to change the past!
And he got this time power how?
I hear it was payment for teaming up with some alien on an insurance scam.
ens and urance cams?
If you weren't so scared, I'd say you were lying. But you are really scared, aren't you?
I'd have to say that I'm sufficiently scared, yes.
Good. Now tell me about how the Puppet Master plans to change the past.

Sixteen blocks away...
The chats I've been monitoring say the alien's name was the Gray Guest.
"The Puppet Master controlled an interplanetary judge, having him sign off on some judicial waivers, totally exonerating the Gray Guest from a whole string of crimes.
"In return, the Gray Guest gave the Puppet Master a small supply of dark matter, an untouched substance from the Big Bang, which plays havoc with time.
"The Puppet Mas has learned to a it to his clay, mo properly, use it his own purpose
"After making puppets from the time-bending dark matter, he was able to use them in order to create an initial connection, and then steal the Invaders from the past."
With the Invaders here, in close proximity to him, he can establish full control over them.
To fight for him?
No. At le not in tod world
Too many heroes these days. Instea the Puppet Master p to return the Invad to the past, to con that world and prepa for the future, mean today's world.

here the
pet Master
an reign
preme."
Who was that?
Calls himself the Amazing Mr. Internets. He has an astonishing amount of information, as long as you don't trust him too much.
I see. Umm--
Steve...
ow are you,
ere, in the future?
It's good. It's good for me. There's a lot of work to be done. The world has become more complex.
You're coming back home with us, though, when this is done. Right?
Elizabeth... when I saw you again it was...it was incredible. It felt like home.
Then you should--
But this is home now, too.
Oh.
I'm not sure what I should do.
I feel like I'm being pulled in two directions.

Two hours later...
Don't let him activate that doll!
If he gets control of Captain America, we lose this battle!
True, but I'm not too sure we win it anyway!
I'm still saying we should have waited for the other Avengers!
The Hulk would be nice right now! He punches things real good!
Unnnh!
We couldn't wait for the other Avengers! When we found the Puppet Master's hideout, we needed to hit fast and hard!
THWUMPT

I know! I know! It's just that I'm allergic to being personally hit fast and hard!
Also...yikes! I'm allergic to getting hit with a fireball!
Don't they have pills for allergies here in the future?
Hey! New girl! I'm the team jokester! You just find a way to stop the Whizzer!
eh eh
It's rather rie to not hear e Sub-Mariner oasting about ow powerful he is!
We could, unfff, do it for him! He is remarkably strong!
Spider-Man! Webbing every-where! Like the plan!
Webbing everywhere?
What can I say? I'm the guy they call when someone needs a mess!

Or when you need to make it really hard to run at super speed!
Unfff!
You caught the Whizzer!
heh heh
Human Torch! Toro! Burn him free of the webbing!
No. I don't think so.
BRANKKK
THUNPPT
Get 'em while they're down!
Now all we need to do is fight a guy who's almost as strong as the Hulk! Tell you what, you go first!
Yes you do! You're always rude!

Actually, I'll go first!
SPAKKTT
No!

You fools! You've destroyed Sub-Mariner puppet, eby restoring his mind d sending him back to his own time!
Actually, that doesn't sound very foolish to me.
Sounds like an excellent idea.

Torch is waking up!
So is Toro, and we're running dry on the fire extinguishers!!

Get those dolls!
No! You can't have them!!

Sorry, chuckles, but spider strength beats bald guy strength.

KAAY RUNNCH

They're gone!
I've got the Whizzer's puppet!
heh heh

And that's that.
When we get back to Avengers Tower, we'll destroy the puppets for you two, and everything will be back to normal.

There's still this one.
Oh, right. That one.

So...what do we do with it?
It was never activated.

You know, I think we could activate it ourselves, and then smash it, and that would very probably return you to the past, to your own time, with us.
I... but--
SNIKT
SNAKKTT
Hey!
orry. But world of day needs ou more.
You... you--
You're probably right, old friend.
Sure I am. The world of today needs you here.
In fact, let's just consider this as me doing my part for community service, okay?
...end

#38
2009
SOTO
COLOR
.COM

Owww!
Caleb! Quit that! This is the wrong time for this!
If she doesn't want her hair pulled, she should quit wearing pigtails.
If you don't want your face smacked, you should quit saying stupid--
Hey!
WHUMPPFF
Caleb! Dang it! No!
Knock it off or the guardian will get mad!
Whoopee. The guuuuuardian.
What's he going to do?
Well...

LUKE CAGE
STORM
SPIDER-MAN
ANT-MAN
HULK
...I could EAT you.
TOUGH-SKINNED MAMA
WEATHER GODDES
SPIDER-POWERED WEB-
PINT-SIZED SCIENT
SUPER-STRONG ALTER
SCIENTIST BRUCE BA
TOGETHER THEY AR
WORLD'S MIGHTIEST H
BATTLING THE FO
NO SINGLE SUPER
COULD WITHST
THE AVENGE
Ahh. Ahhhhh. Ahhh.
I'll be good.
MS. ISAACSON'S THIRD GRADE FIELD T
PAUL TOBIN – WRITER JACOPO CAMAGNI – ARTIST SOTOCOLOR – COLORS DAVE SHARPE – LETT
JONES & SOTOMAYOR – COVER PAUL ACERIOS – PRODUCTION RALPH MACCHIO – CONSULTING NATHAN COSBY – E
JOE QUESADA – EDITOR IN CHIEF DAN BUCKLEY – PUBLISHER ALAN FINE – EXECUTIVE PRODUCER

VE HOURS EARLIER...
Good! Uh, to meet you. It's good. Sorry... I'm a little nervous!
When I had the children enter the essay contest, I knew there was supposed to be a special grand prize--
WELCOME AVENGE
--but I never dreamed it would be a day with the Avengers!
They're here! The Avengers are here!
es! This rules!
Hulk! Stay off the monkey bars!
Ben Dewey.
I'm Emmella Isaacson.
My name is Ororo, or Storm if you like.
I'm Ant-Man!
And of course you know Spider-Man.
Oh. Geez. We will totally pay for the damage to the monkey bars.
Hulk is sorry for the breaky things.
It happens. You wouldn't believe what these children can destroy. I'm just glad the four of you could make it here.
Five of us, hopefully.
Luke Cage is supposed to be here.
WHIRRRRRR

Five of us, hopefully. Luke Cage is supposed to be here.
Your friends are waiting for you, Mr. Luke Cage. So sorry that my plans have interrupted your own.
Seriously, Mandarin, how do you type when your fingernails are like that?
Ahh. Spirit! Good! Even when your situation is hopeless, you continue to struggle.
Such is your strength.
And that strength will soon be mine.
Siphoned into the Cyclone, a robot of my own design.
A robot? Here I thought you were all about your fancy rings.
These? Admirable weapons indeed, but I find it amusing to defeat th Avengers using their own powers.

I think using the *robot* means you're just too *chicken* to fight on your *own!* Let *me* down from here and I'll--
--be weak as a *child.* Did you not *hear?* The siphoner has been *prepared.*
In moments, the Cyclone will have your *prodigious* strength at its disposal.
In turn, each Avenger will fall prey, and the powers of each fallen Avenger will be added to the Cyclone, until the Mighty Avengers are no more.
I'll start *small,* of course. That's why I picked *you.*
Funny. If I'm so *small*--
-how come you eded to attack me when I was leep? Hit me with nockout gas? y didn't you just--

Play fair?
Please tell me that you were about to ask why I didn't play fair.
Because if that's what you were going to say, I have an answer for you.
It's because I'm the bad guy.
Arrghh! This...this isn't going to work, you know!
Won't work? I assure you, I've employed the finest scientists to--
NO! I mean... ARRGHH...the Avengers!
When I don't show up, they'll know something's wrong! They'll be on alert!
They'll come looking for m
because they k
that only the wo
of villains cou
keep me from
It is becoming late. Perhaps we should continue without Luke?
Yeah. He probably got a call from his mom, or something. Sometimes those calls take hours.
That woman is straight up nefarious.
HA HA HA HA HA! HA HA HA HA
Unhhh.

Okay, children, ow that we've split ff into groups, and nt the rest of your lassmates off with e other Avengers, we can get started.
We're oing to learn eteorology-- at's the study f weather-- from Storm.
Why is it called meteorology, not like, weatherology, or something like that?
Excellent question. The answer goes back to the early days of science, when meteors were actually thought to be a part of the Earth's weather system.
So, meteorology is rather a misnomer.
What's a misnomer?
Another excellent question. But would you rather talk about words, or perhaps--
--watch me call lightning from the skies?
Ohhh!
Whoa!
Neat!
Sweeeet!
Or fly with the aid of precisely controlled winds?
Awesome!

Or... you could watch Storm succumb to my Cyclone robot. Would you like that, children?
THE MANDARIN!!
Children, RUN!
Yes, children. Do run. Except for you.
Ahhh!
This is precisely why I have chosen this day to enact my plans.
You Avengers will be forced to hold back, for fear of hurting the dear children. I, of course, have no such qualms.
A robot? You're using a robot? This is unlike you!
Let me go!
Your friend Luke Cage felt the same way. I told him that--

Luke? You have Luke?
I do. You'll meet him soon enough.
In fact, you can meet a part of him right now.
Your meaning?
His formidable strength now resides in the Cyclone's titanium frame.
NK
TINK
TINK
My winds! My lightning! No effect!
Of course not. With the Cyclone's built-in defense measures combined with Cage's strength it can--

I cannot win this fight! I must--
Ut ut ut. A moment. Aren't you forgetting the children?
The children!
Unnhh!!
Unnuuu--
--the children--

EWHERE...
Okay, now anybody that can do *this,* doesn't have to wear a safety harness during their climbs.
Now, *who's first?*
*Me!* I'm geared up! *Me! Me!*
Sweet. And I'm climbing along with you, so there's no reason to be afraid of falling off.
I'm *not* afraid of falling off, 'cuz I've got a *harness.* I'm a little afraid of *you* falling off, though.
*Me?*
*Ooof!*
Yeah. Cuz you're really *weird.*
Dunno.
Weird *good* or weird *bad?*
Fantastic. The tension's *unbearable.* Now put some *muscle* into it. Keep *climbing.* Up. *Up!*
mb! You're *ost* there! u can *do* it!
Let me help you.
*Ufff!* Thanks!
*Huh?* My *danger sense?*

The MANDARIN!
And friend.
Ahh!
Put her down, Mandarin!
And I'm not your friend!
As I am no friend of yours, dear child. By "friend," I was referring to the Cyclone robot.
The what?
Whoa! What the--?
It is a robot. One with the strength of Luke Cage, and now Storm's mutant ability to control the weather.
Rather invigorating winds, are they not? With winds such as these, it's a splendid day to defeat the Avengers, or, perhaps--

AHHHH!
--to fly a kite.
Mr. ider-Man! Help!
m sorry alled you weird!
Mandarin! Leave the children out of this! This is between you and me!
No. This is about defeating you, and the child is an efficient means to that end.
For instance, she has distracted you from the Cyclone.
WHUMMPFF
Unnggghh!
And, just like Storm, you were afraid to use your full powers.

This from fear of endangering the children.
But do not fret. Your full powers will indeed be used.
When I have them.
Unconscious? Good. Today's schedule is demanding.
I must drain you of your powers and instill them in the Cyclone.
Introduce you children to a dragon.
And then be off to the petting zoo.

NE HOUR LATER, AT
HE PETTING ZOO.
Bunnies
get scared.
All people be
gentle.
Important
for being quiet.
Big noises worry
nice animals.
Animals sense how
children feel. If children
scared...animals
scared.
Happy
children
make happy
animals.
Horses
like to be
held.
Let's go
ee the dogs
with funny
sweaters.
The
what?
I think
he means
sheep.

Hulk likes the *fuzzy* doggies.
They're called *sheep.*
Hulk likes the *sheepdogs.*
No. A *sheepdog* is *still* a *dog,* these are--

Excuse me. It's the *sheep's birthday.* Hulk, would you *blow out* the *candles?*
*Cake!*
Wait.

The Mandarin? Yes.

*Hulk!* Don't *blow out the candles!*
*Huh?* Why Hulk *not?* Hulk...uhhh.

Hulk *dizzy.*
What's *going on?* What are you *doing?*
Oh, it's an *attack,* but due to the Hulk's *raw power* I did not dare attack with *force.*

Instead, I had *blow out* candles. *tying* his *lungs* of And then, at *that* moment--
--this robot used *Storm's mutant abilities* to *vacuum* even *more* air away from the Hulk, keeping any *additional* oxygen from reaching his lungs.
He's *suffocating.* The *mighty Hulk,* felled by *wind* and a *birthday cake.*
Rather *exciting,* wasn't it?
And now, I'll have to ask you and the children to accompany me.
Children, I think we better do as he says.

Why did he need us? Why bring us here?
Hostages. He needs hostages. Or maybe he just likes to scare kids with a dragon.
Why does he have a dragon?
Because dragons are symbols of strength and power. Quite fitting for today.
For you were invited not as hostages, but rather as witnesses to an important event, one long overdue.
The END of the AVENGERS!
All their powers have now been siphoned! The Cyclone is all of what they once were!
And now, Cyclone--

FFFWHOOSSH
What?!! Ungghh!
Huh? Yeah!
Cyclone! You dare turn against me?!
Yeah. I do. I'm rather daring!

It talks?
Well... it doesn't talk.

I do! Ant-Man!

I'm inside this crazy thing! It's rather an ingenious construct!
You're inside the robot?!

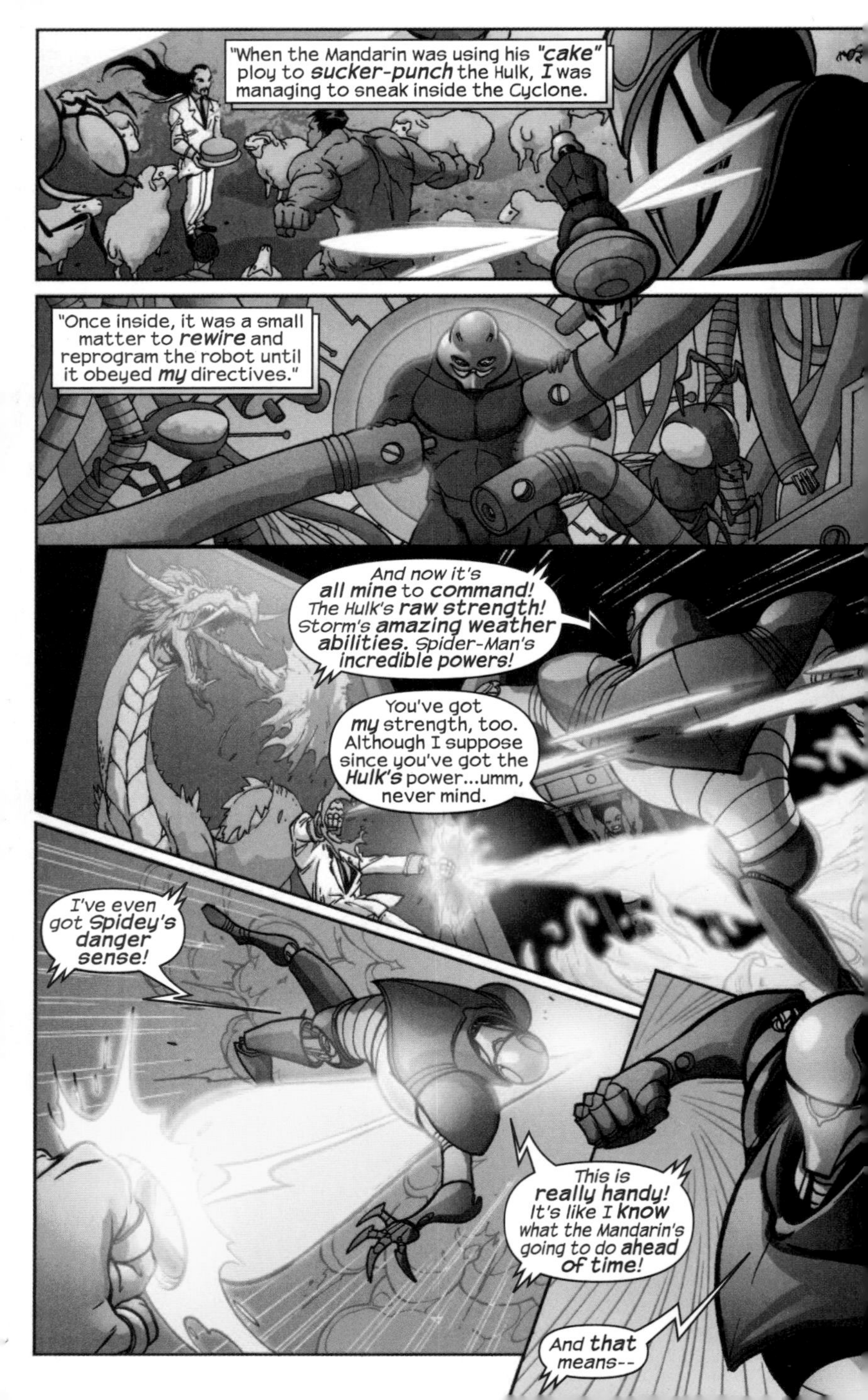
"When the Mandarin was using his "cake" ploy to sucker-punch the Hulk, I was managing to sneak inside the Cyclone.
"Once inside, it was a small matter to rewire and reprogram the robot until it obeyed my directives."
And now it's all mine to command! The Hulk's raw strength! Storm's amazing weather abilities. Spider-Man's incredible powers!
You've got my strength, too. Although I suppose since you've got the Hulk's power...umm, never mind.
I've even got Spidey's danger sense!
This is really handy! It's like I know what the Mandarin's going to do ahead of time!
And that means--

THWAKKT
THUNKKT
I know you're going down!
Actually, no. I can't predict the future. My power doesn't work that way.

Don't ruin my big lines! I'm the one doing all the fighting...I should get to say whatever I want!
And, speaking of me doing all the ...hting...I figured out ...ow to give everyone their powers back!

Hulk Smash!

I think not. This battle is lost.
I'll take my leave.

The dragon is vanishing as well!
Haw!
Owww!

I will call and let your school know that you and the children are *safe.*
We'll get everyone *home.*
It's not *time* to *go home* yet.
Yeah...we're *supposed* to have a *whole day* with the Avengers!
The kids are *right.* We'd be *cheating* them.
Now, who wants to list to a *detaile explanation* o I *defeated* t *Mandarin?*
Or, if you kids want, you could *come with me* and *I'll* show you my *two* powers.
*Two* powers?
That's right. I'm *super* strong, *and* I can *find all the best ice cream parlors!*
*Yay!*
*Ooooo-kay!*
Did he say ice cream? I'm going with them!
Please turn off the lights when you're done here, Ant-Man.
May I be excused?
...END

#39

CENTRAL PARK, N.Y.C.
Here's the rules. We race each other through Central Park. No tripping. No tackling. No tickling.
And whoever wins gets these front row tickets to the United States versus Japan All-Star baseball game.
Exactly. And you can't use your webbing.
Yes, I can. And you can't throw things at me.
But I will. Ready?
Oh yeah.
On the count of three.
One!
Two!
WEEET
WEEET
WEEET
Wait! My phone!
Serious
Your pho
Is this sc
spide
trick
Shush.
What's going on?
Some guy pleading for help. Says he's been kidnapped. Forced to commit a crime.
They're making me steal things from an army base!
Is this for real?
Let me get this straight...at this very moment you're sneaking onto an army base?
Sneaki

SPIDER-MAN
TIGRA
STORM
WOLVERINE
LUKE CAGE
PIDER-POWERED WEB-SLINGER. CAT-LIKE CRUSADER. WEATHER GODDESS. FERAL MUTANT BRAWLER. TOUGH-SKINNED MAMA'S BOY. TOGETHER THEY ARE THE WORLD'S MIGHTIEST HEROES, BATTLING THE FOES THAT NO SINGLE SUPER HERO COULD WITHSTAND!
E AVENGERS
No. We're not exactly sneaking.
DON'T FOLLOW THE LEADER
PAUL TOBIN WRITER
HORACIO DOMINGUES PENCILER
CRAIG YEUNG INKER SOTOCOLOR COLORS
DAVE SHARPE LETTERER JONES & SOTO COVER
PAUL ACERIOS PRODUCTION RALPH MACCHIO CONSULTING
NATHAN COSBY EDITOR JOE QUESADA EDITOR IN CHIEF
DAN BUCKLEY PUBLISHER ALAN FINE EXECUTIVE PRODUCER

TWO HOURS LATER.
So, some of the soldiers we talked to said the Rhino was a part of this, and some of them said he wasn't.
And most of them gave me their phone numbers.

It's actually rather hard to tell how *much* of a part the Rhino played in this attack.
You'll see what I mean in these *tapes.*
"Look here. The Abomination is busting through the outside wall, and there's the Rhino right behind him.

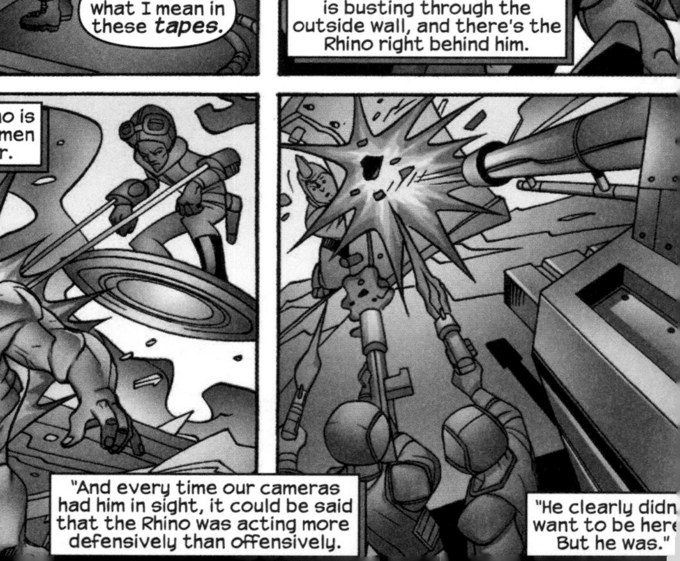
"But here the Rhino is saving two of my men from the Leader.
"And every time our cameras had him in sight, it could be said that the Rhino was acting more defensively than offensively.
"He clearly didn
want to be here
But he was."

You say the o called you to j he was being coerced?
Yep. Kidnapped. Forced into a life of crime.
Of course, he was already leading a life of crime, so we're a bit confused.

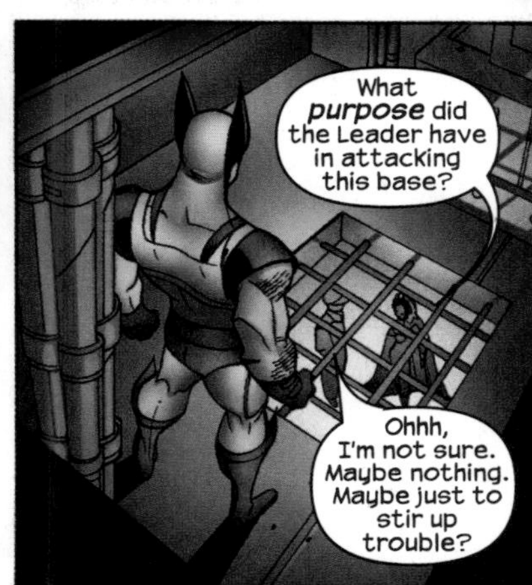
What purpose did the Leader have in attacking this base?
Ohhh, I'm not sure. Maybe nothing. Maybe just to stir up trouble?

Wrong. Maybe Abomination thinks ting up army bases a cool hobby, but the eader is a man with a purpose.
He wanted something. What was it?
I'm afraid that information is classified under the federal--
You kidding me? I have Avengers level access.
I'm authorized to know anything and everything, from what underwear you put on this morning to whatever it is that the Leader stole, so save me a phone call and tell me the truth.
The truth about the Leader, not that under-wear thing.

If you think you can come onto a U.S. Army base and threaten me with--
BEEP
BOOP
BIP
Ahhh, dang. What a day. It was satellite codes.

Satellite codes? The Leader isn't going to be messing with my *satellite television,* is he?
Because the *World Sumo Championships* are--
We're talking *military* satellites. *Secret* ones.

And these secret military satellites, what do they *do?*
Well, there are several of them, and they each have lasers.
And these lasers, how *powerful* are they?
Not *too* powerful. At least, not unless they're *combined.*
This is where you tell us the Leader can combine them now, isn't it?

"With all of the codes the Leader now has, he could, umm, align them into a single laser capable of wiping out... oh...a small town."

A small town? The laser could blast a small town?
And what is your *definition* of a *small town?*
Oh. Umm. Ahh...about the size of maybe... *Chicago?*
Did he just say *Chicago?*
Yes. I fear that he did.
So we have a *huge* aser in the *sky,* and it's ow controlled by a *mad* nius and *two* of the *world's* rongest *villains,* although one of them claims to be *kidnapped.*
Why do *I* always get these jobs?
Because Iron Man hogs all the missions with rainbows and winged puppies.
*Dang!*
Wolverine, I hope *you're* finding something, because getting this general to talk is like pulling *candy-coated teeth* from a *baby.*

Yeah. I found something interesting just sorta lying around in a vault.
*Grab it. We'll meet you back at the Quinjet.*

SOON. IN THE QUINJET.
What did you find?
Looks like ham sandwiches. Turkey sandwiches. Roast beef sandwiches. Jeez, even olive loaf.
Yeah...I sn in a little tri the commiss Some goo eating.

But chomp your eyes on this.
Whoa. These are schematics for the laser array.
Chomp your eyes on this? What does that even mean?

The Leader must know he's on a tig deadline. The acce codes are difficult reset, but it shoul take more than a day.

That means he has to make his move soon.
He'll be-- ahh! I see how this works.

Storm. I've got an important job for you.
Of course. Just tell me what you wish.

HOUR LATER.
So how do we find the Leader?
And how do we find a better hot dog? This one tastes like a donkey.
WESTMINSTER'S
ing the Leader could ve problematic. Next Reed Richards, he's bably the smartest man alive.
Right. And that makes him good at hiding.
If I cooked hot dogs like this, I'd go into hiding.
Good thing you have this umbrella.
Yeah. It's getting cloudy. Wasn't it supposed to be sunny all day?
And hot dogs are supposed to taste good. Know what I'm sayin'?
Jeez, Wolverine... didn't you just eat about half that army base's rations?

My mutant healing factor makes for a fast metabolism. I get hungry. Got a problem with that?
Gosh no, Mr. Scary Man. And these hot dogs taste fine to me.
Are you demented? I could do a better job cooking these things! A schnauzer could do a better job! An insect! Even Spider-Man!
I think I was insulted somewhere in there.
Yeah. Let's mess with him.

I bet you twenty dollars Spider-Man can cook a better hot dog than you.
You're on! Hand me the spices and stand back!

I'll take two.
Two, please.
Can he wear the apron?

CLICK CLICK CLICK
I'm having Iron Man track down all suspicious sales of tech equipment. Hopefully we can chase down the Leader that way.
I've got feelers out to some of my under-world contacts. Somebody will know some-thing.

You have underworld contacts?
A couple ex-boyfriends. They were nice back when I was dating them.
I'd best reserve comments.

So how 'bout them hot dogs? Pretty good, eh? Now it's your turn, Spidey.
I'll pass. You win.
I just can't take the chance of my friends taking photos of me wearing an apron and putting them online, the way we're going to do with you.
Huh?

You know I'm going to get back at you guys for this.
What can I say? I live for the present.
And speaking of the present, we need to deal with the Leader.
Let's get a plan, people. It's not like the bad guys are going to give us a call and tell us what's up.
SHRING SHRING
Whoop. My phone.
EEP EEP
Ooo. Mine too.
Hmmm.
I always feel so left out when friends are talking on cell phones.
I could give you a call, if it would make you feel better.
That was one of my admirers from the army base. According to him, they just received a call from the Leader.
He's demanding a quarter trillion dollars, or he'll devastate New York.
That is not good.
My call was from the Rhino. He wants us to know he's not a part of this, and he's currently uploading all the information on where they are, and what they're doing.
We can stop this.
And that is good.

There are *three* different locations.
Probably a *redundancy* factor, so that if any *one* of them gets taken down, then the *threat* remains.

That means we'll have to take down *all three* of them.
*Luke,* you and *Wolverine* stop the *Abomination.*
Can do.
Can at least *try.*

I'm off to take down the *Leader!*
Be careful!

Okay. I guess I'll just take on the Rhino *all by myself* then.

TY MINUTES LATER.
Wolverine! I can't keep him away from the laser satellite's trigger device!
Get your claws over here!

I can't even get close to him!
You guys are just too precious!
You wanna fight with the Abomination, you should 'a brought the Hulk!
I mean, what is this? A dainty punk and a runt with ice picks for knuckles?
Wolverine's got more than ice picks.

Yeah? What else?
Well, he's real *sneaky.* He stole the satellite trigger when you weren't looking.
That I *did.*

Wha...?

Give that back!
And *another* thing Wolverine has--

--is a me
*skeleton*
of the *har*
*substa*
in the *kn*
*univers*
Huh?

Hey!

Oommpf!
Uhhnnn!

The
tal is called
amantium.

It hurts, *don't* it?
THUMMPTT

You *could* have let me in on this little *battle strategy* of yours.

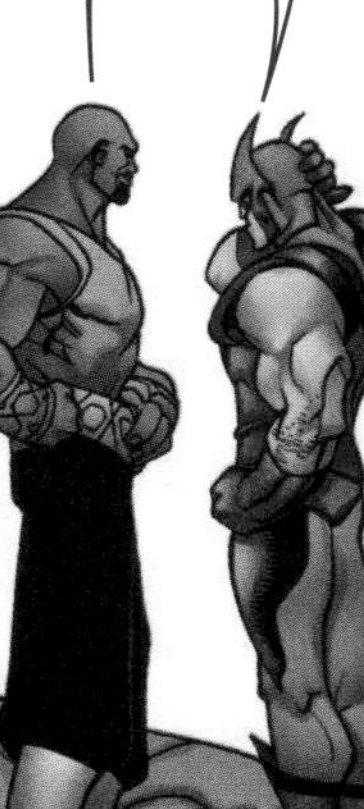
Oh. *Sorry.* Is it *too late?*
Because if *not*...then, *hey*... would you mind me *using* you like a *club* to take down the *Abomination?*
Sure. Why *not?* Whatever *works.*

DOWNTOWN.
I just don't see how this is going to work.
So! You've gained the Power Cosmic? Then I have no chance!
Huh? What are you tal about?
Oooff!
Got you! Now, despite you having harnessed the power of a million exploding suns, despite how you have summoned this fierce thunderstorm, the Rhino will triumph!
Have you gone insane?

Work with me, here. I want out of the villain business. No long-term gain, and I feel like a jerk hurting people.
But...if this is going to be my final battle, I'd at least like to go out with a bang.
Oh. I get it. Don't want to get beat up by a tiny ol' girl, huh?

Uhh, yeah. Sorry. I got an image to protect. I was hoping you guys would send the Hulk.
Well, maybe not the Hulk. Let's say... Spider-Man.
One... two, and

ra
aks
e!
No mere mortal can hold this child of the stars!
No! This can't be!
Now you will pay a dire price for challenging the very daughter of the universe!
Arrgh! Such power!
THOOONT
How am I doing?
ot bad.
sound a bit
a hippie,
though.
Oooo.
Sorry. You
ady for the
nockout
blow?
Yep. Go.
It's clobberin' time!
KWUUMPFF
Tigra, this is Luke. Everything going okay, there?
For sure! Won the fight. Stole a line from the Thing.
I'm totally a hero, and everything's fine.
Except for this rain. I hate it when my fur gets wet.

NEW YORK SHIPYARDS.
My sensors tell me that I am now the last of the three. As ever, the Leader stands alone.
Well, alone except for that rockin' battle suit you made. Don't suppose you'd take it off and really stand alone, would you?

Yow! Okay, okay!
Well, I don't suppose that thing short circuits in the rain, does it?
ZREEEEEEN
Rain? This exoskeleton is capable of complete submersion!
This storm is indeed fierce, but my armor could withstand far worse extremes! It could--
Right. Right. I got it. You don't need to do the full sales pitch. I'm not trying to buy the thing!
Not unless you take if off and let me have a test drive!

render at once, or I trigger the satellite ser array, and New rk will pay the price.

You know I can't do that.
You have no choice.

You're right. on't have a choice. ere's no way I can et you walk away from here.
I won't do that.

You say that I'm joking while New York hangs by a thread, but listen to me, understand what I'm saying.

I'm not joking.
You're not walking away from here.

Spider-Man?
Stay back. I KNOW what I'm doing.
Ahh, the rest of your team arrives. So be it.

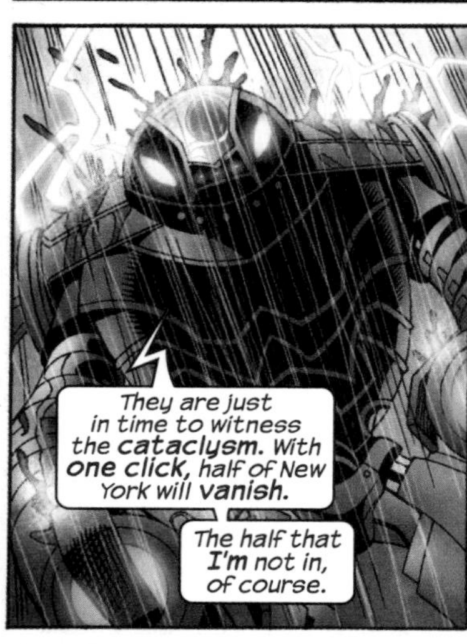
They are just in time to witness the cataclysm. With one click, half of New York will vanish.
The half that I'm not in, of course.

CLICK

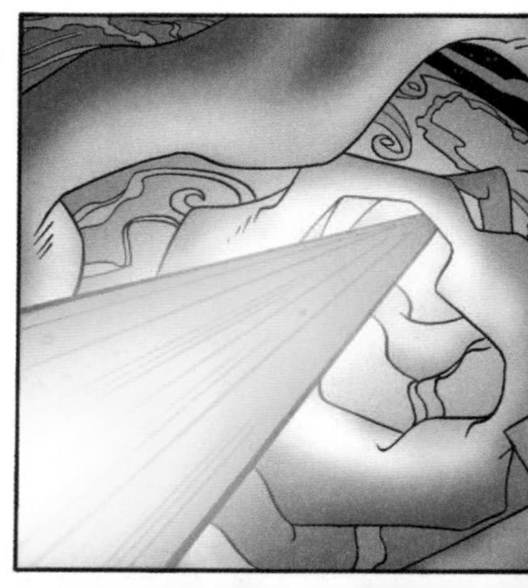

Why...why did it not work?

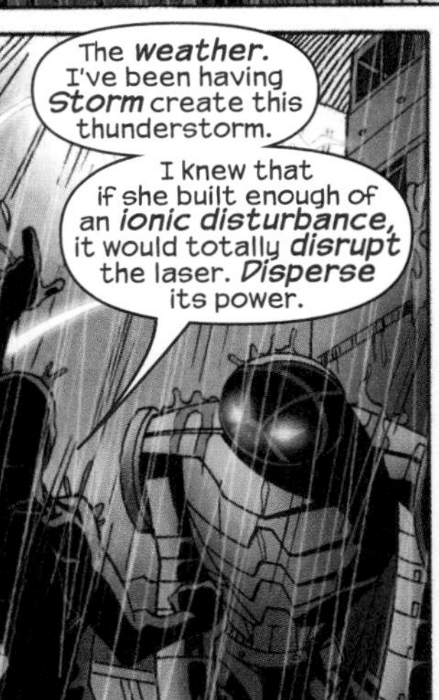
The weather. I've been having Storm create this thunderstorm.
I knew that if she built enough of an ionic disturbance, it would totally disrupt the laser. Disperse its power.

Simply put, I outsmarted you. And I beat you. All thanks to Storm.

KRAAAKKOOOOOOOOM
You've met Storm, haven't you?

How's all your high tech equipment working now, smart guy?
My circuits! They're all fused! I can't move! I'm helpless!
Yeah. We're mean that way.
Great work with the storm, Storm.
Thank you. Shall I let the skies clear now?
Yeah! Because Tigra and I still ne to race to see wh wins the basebal tickets!
First one back to Avengers Tower wins!
You'r on

Who do you think will win?
Doesn't matter much.

I stole the tickets from Spider-Man. They're mine now.
I told guys I'd you ba

AY LATER.
So, the Rhino was able to go free after our testimony of how he helped stop the Leader.
Right. And Iron Man used his connections to get him a job.
Official mascot for Japan's all-star team.
Once we found out that their team nickname was the Rhinos, it seemed like a given.
RHINOS

Yep. All in all, m pretty happy ith how this one turned out.

Who wants a t-shirt! Who wants a t-shirt!
Here's some for my friends in the front row!

And here's one for the other guys!
These seats reek!
Ummphh!
...END